A Right Royal Mess

'A Right Royal Mess'
An original concept by Rachel Lyon
© Rachel Lyon

Illustrated by Catalina Echeverri

Published by MAVERICK ARTS PUBLISHING LTD

Studio 3A, City Business Centre, 6 Brighton Road,

Horsham, West Sussex, RH13 5BB

© Maverick Arts Publishing Limited July 2017

+44 (0)1403 256941

A CIP catalogue record for this book is available at the British Library.

ISBN 978-1-84886-298-2

arts publishing
www.maverickbooks.co.uk

This book is rated as: Purple Band (Guided Reading)
The original picture book text for this story has been
modified by the author to be an early reader.

A Right Royal MeSS

By Rachel Lyon

Illustrated by Catalina Echeverri

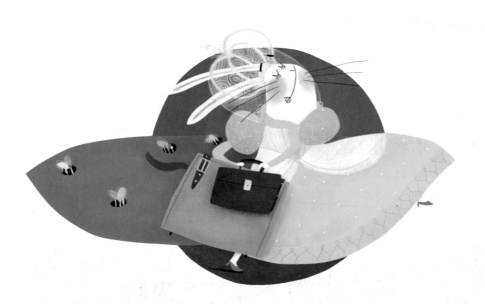

Queen Fluff was a very fancy bunny.

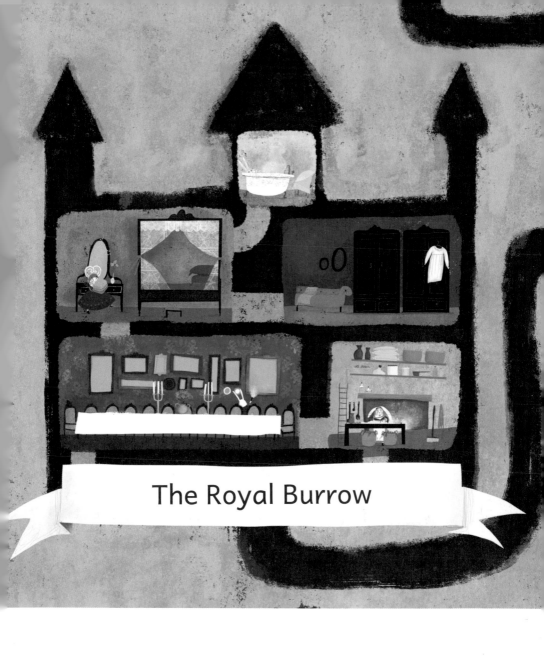

The Royal Burrow

She always wore a big fancy crown,

and lived in a big fancy burrow.

Even though she had plenty of money,

Queen Fluff had no friends at all.

Not one. She was lonely and bored.

One day she had an idea. "I will go and visit all the bunnies in my Kingdom," she said. "When I find the bunny with the fanciest burrow, I'll stay with them for a week."

So Queen Fluff sent a letter to every bunny in the Kingdom. She ordered them to make their burrows fancy, and to cook her a fancy feast.

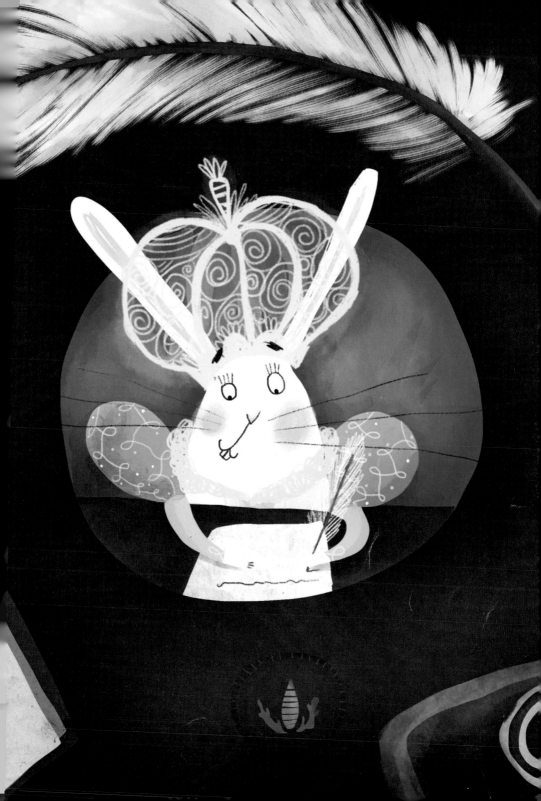

But the other bunnies in the kingdom were poor. They couldn't afford fancy things.

"Queen Fluff must be very thoughtless," they said. "Let's teach her a lesson!" So the bunnies worked very hard, getting ready for the Queen's visit.

They collected all the smelliest, yuckiest things they could find. They put all the smelly, yucky things in their burrows.

The Queen was busy too, getting ready for her trip. She couldn't wait to see the other bunnies' burrows and choose which was the fanciest.

The Royal Burrow

Bunnyshire

When the big day came, she set off in her fancy

royal coach.

When the bunnies saw her arrive, they giggled.

What would the Queen think of their messy,

smelly burrows?

The Queen ran eagerly

into the first burrow.

But the only thing waiting for her was a swarm of bees!

"Yawoooh!" she yelped, as the bees stung her on her furry bottom. "That's no way to treat a Queen!"

The next burrow was even worse!

It was full of toads and creepy-crawlies.

"Some lunch, my lady?" asked the bunnies

inside, offering her a bowl of slug soup.

"Yuck!" said the Queen, and she ran

straight off to the next burrow.

Plop! The Queen slid down into the burrow, and landed in a big pile of muck!

"My shiny gold slippers are ruined!"

she wailed.

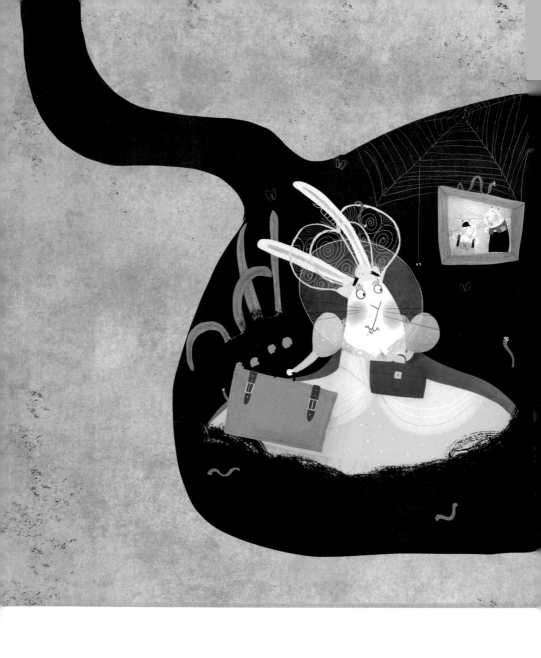

There was no one there to greet her except for

a rat... who was wearing only his underpants!

Queen Fluff was fed up. "I'm leaving!" she cried.

"Hooray!" cheered the bunnies. "We did it!

We got rid of thoughtless Queen Fluff!"

But the Queen had heard every word they said.

"Oh dear," said Queen Fluff, taking off her crown.

"I see now. You're right – I have been
thoughtless and unkind. If only there was
a way we could be friends."

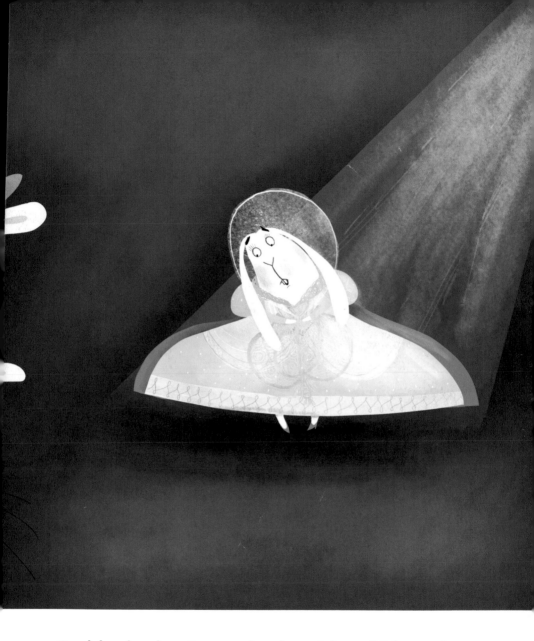

Suddenly the Queen had an idea. "I know!

Why don't you come back to my place for

a party?" she said.

That night, as the bunnies danced and laughed and ate together...

Queen Fluff realised that although fancy burrows and fancy feasts are nice, real friends are far nicer.

Quiz

1. Why is Queen Fluff unhappy?
a) She has lost her birthday cake
b) Her fancy dress was ruined
c) She has no friends

2. What does Queen Fluff want to find?
a) The fanciest burrow
b) A new crown
c) A gold slipper

3. Why do the other bunnies want to trick Queen Fluff?
a) Because they think she is thoughtless
b) Because they want to sleep in her burrow
c) Because they want to eat her carrots

4. What does Queen Fluff find in the burrows?

a) Gold crowns

b) Smelly, mucky things

c) Fancy parties

5. How does Queen Fluff become friends with the other bunnies?

a) She buys them all new burrows

b) She cooks them a feast

c) She invites them to a party

Turn over for answers

Book Bands for Guided Reading

The Institute of Education book banding system is a scale of colours that reflects the various levels of reading difficulty. The bands are assigned by taking into account the content, the language style, the layout and phonics.

Maverick Early Readers are a bright, attractive range of books covering the pink to purple bands. All of these books have been book banded for guided reading to the industry standard and edited by a leading educational consultant.

For more titles visit:
www.maverickbooks.co.uk/early-readers

 Pink

 Red

 Yellow

 Blue

 Green

 Orange

 Turquoise

 Purple

Book Band Purple

A Right Royal Mess	978-1-84886-298-2
Stone Underpants	978-1-84886-297-5
Biscuit Blast Off!	978-1-84886-236-4
The Great Grizzly Race	978-1-84886-239-5
The Jelly That Wouldn't Wobble	978-1-84886-225-8

Quiz Answers: 1c, 2a, 3a, 4b, 5c